Cardinal

Zoe

Father

Robin

Wren

Sky

to Ripper
from
Bev & NANA

FLY HIGH

MICHELLE MEDLOCK ADAMS and **JANET K. JOHNSON**

illustrated by **BETH SNIDER**

Gracie and Bennett loved helping Mama fill the bird feeders and clean the bird bath.

Every day, more birds visited their backyard. Doves. Robins. Sparrows. Wrens. Pigeons. Red-winged Blackbirds. Blue Jays. Cardinals. Even the occasional Downy Woodpecker.

But Cardinals were Gracie's favorite.

. . . .

Long before we were born, everything was created. Day and night, the oceans and dry land, even the plants and trees. Trees with flowers and all the different fruits made the earth so pretty. Then the animals, fish, and birds came, and people helped to take care of it all.

Do you take care of a pet, a stuffed animal, or a baby brother or sister?

. . . .

"Look!" Mama said. "Do you see them?"

"See what?" Bennett asked.

"The baby birds! There are three of them."

Gracie ran into the house, grabbed her binoculars,
and bolted back to her mother's side.

"I'm gonna watch over the baby birds until their mama returns," Gracie announced.

Just like baby birds need help until they grow strong enough to feed themselves, we have our family to help us. Sometimes there's a mom and dad. Sometimes just a mom or a dad. Other times it may be grandparents, aunts, uncles, or someone else who becomes our family.

Who watches over you and keeps you safe?

That night, Gracie worried.

"I never saw the mama bird return to her nest and I watched a long time."

"I'm sure she was just out getting food for her babies," Mama said. "Sleep tight, sweetie."

But Gracie couldn't sleep.

Sometimes we feel something is wrong.

Can you think of a time when you felt that something was wrong even before you knew what was happening?

That next morning, they found Mama Bird lying outside
the fence. She was hurt.

"Oh no," Gracie cried. "Bennett, go get Mama!"

Mama placed the injured bird in a box and moved her to a safe place. Then she hurried inside to call a veterinarian.

Gracie put her arm around Bennett as they sat next to the box.

When something bad happens, we try to believe everything will be okay. *Shock* and *denial* are often the first stages of grief. We ask "why" over and over trying to make sense of what happened.

When you heard (name of person, pet, or friend) died or was seriously hurt, what feelings did you have?
How do you feel now?

It seemed like hours since Mama had taken the injured bird to the vet.

Gracie kept an eye on the baby birds, while Bennett practiced his best bird calls.

Finally, the back door opened. Mama reached out her arms and pulled Gracie in for a long hug.

"I'm so sorry, sweetie. Dr. Bob did all he could. Sometimes these things just happen."

....

There are times we do not have the answers. What we do know is that we don't need to be afraid of dying.

Sometimes, even if we do everything we can, people and pets still die.

How do you think the mama bird felt knowing someone was caring for her?

....

"I don't understand!" Gracie cried.

Bennett dropped to his knees.

"It's not fair!" he yelled. "Why couldn't the doctor fix her?"

Gracie buried her face in Mama's hug, trying hard to hold back the tears.

....

Shock and *denial* are often followed by *sadness* and *bargaining*. When someone you love dies, you may feel like no one listened to what you wanted or cared about how you felt. The truth is you are loved and people do care how you feel.

....

Bennett kicked over the birdseed container as he
ran into the house. Gracie took off her binoculars
and threw them. They landed next to the empty box.
Then she followed after her brother.

Mama cleaned up the birdseed and picked up the binoculars.

She wasn't mad. She understood.

Often, when we experience loss, we become *angry*. We may act out in a variety of ways because we feel helpless and even blame ourselves for what happened. It's important to understand that it's not your fault.

What did you feel when (name of person, pet, friend) died?

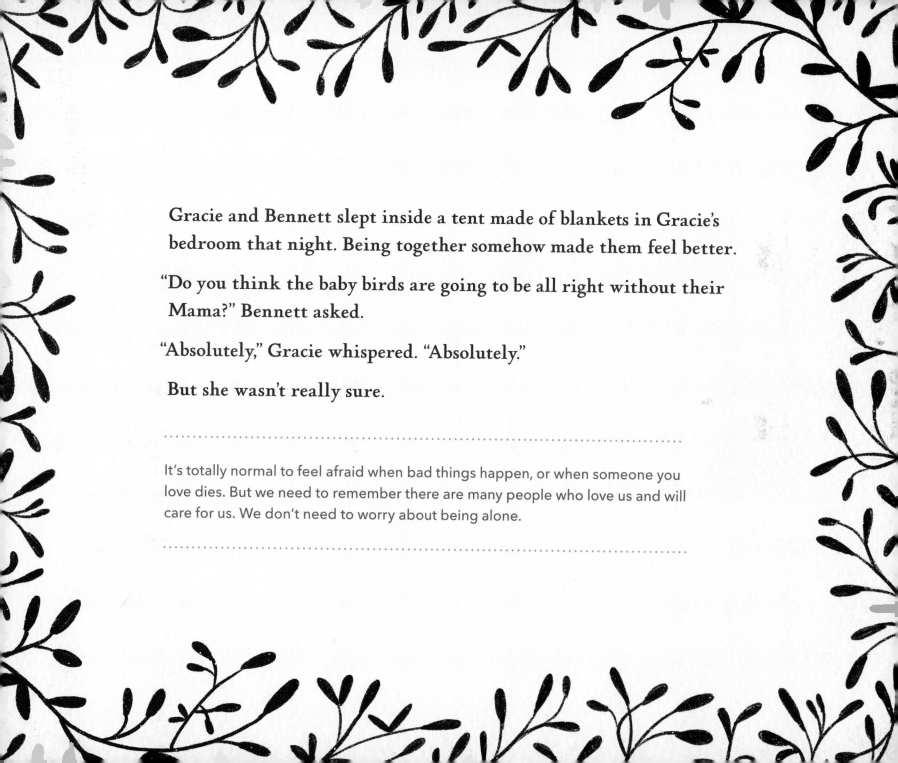

Gracie and Bennett slept inside a tent made of blankets in Gracie's bedroom that night. Being together somehow made them feel better.

"Do you think the baby birds are going to be all right without their Mama?" Bennett asked.

"Absolutely," Gracie whispered. "Absolutely."

But she wasn't really sure.

It's totally normal to feel afraid when bad things happen, or when someone you love dies. But we need to remember there are many people who love us and will care for us. We don't need to worry about being alone.

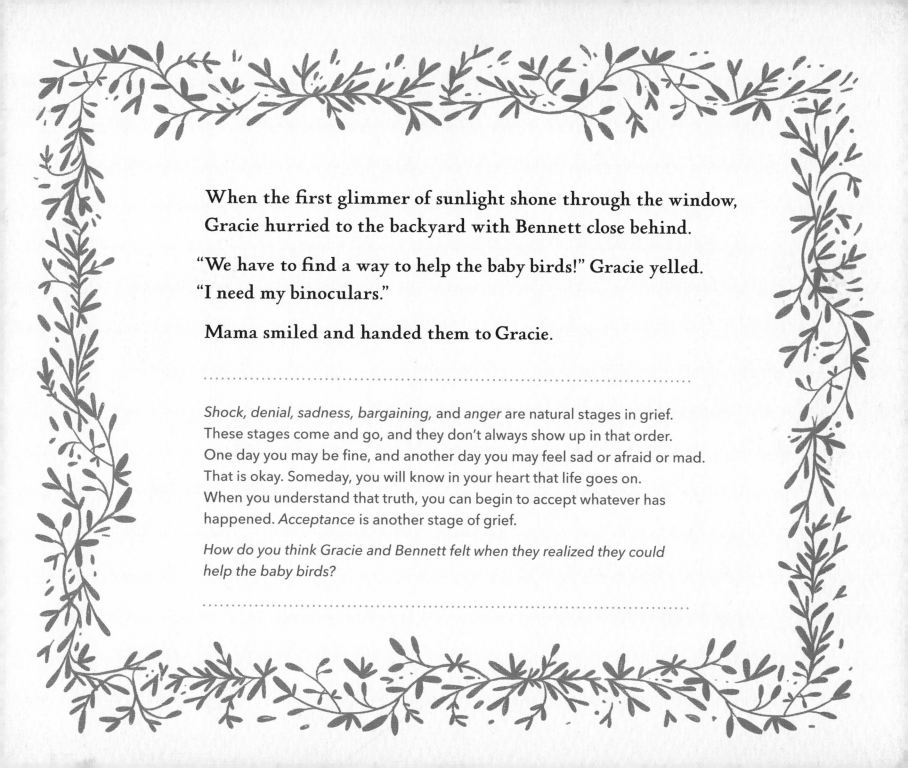

When the first glimmer of sunlight shone through the window, Gracie hurried to the backyard with Bennett close behind.

"We have to find a way to help the baby birds!" Gracie yelled. "I need my binoculars."

Mama smiled and handed them to Gracie.

....

Shock, denial, sadness, bargaining, and *anger* are natural stages in grief. These stages come and go, and they don't always show up in that order. One day you may be fine, and another day you may feel sad or afraid or mad. That is okay. Someday, you will know in your heart that life goes on. When you understand that truth, you can begin to accept whatever has happened. *Acceptance* is another stage of grief.

How do you think Gracie and Bennett felt when they realized they could help the baby birds?

....

Gracie pressed the binoculars to her eyes and gasped.

"The daddy Cardinal is in the nest! He is feeding the baby birds!"

"Let me see! Let me see!" Bennett urged.

Mama, Gracie, and Bennett watched the daddy Cardinal and his babies all day.

He would fly to the suet feeder, peck off a piece of food,
and then fly back to the babies and feed them.

Other times, he would fly to the ground, grab a worm in his beak,
and feed the worm to his babies.

The daddy bird knew what the baby birds needed. He cared for them and taught them how to fly and find food and enjoy life. We can also learn from the people in our lives.

Who helps care for you? What do they do to make sure you are okay? What special memory do you have of the person/pet you lost? Special memories can help us feel less sad.

Gracie and Bennett spent the next few days watching the daddy Cardinal care for his young. They did their part, too. Gracie made sure there was plenty of suet in the feeders. And Bennett made sure the bird bath had lots of water.

Squirt! Squirt! Squirt!

"Watch it!" Gracie called to Bennett. "You're getting me all wet!" Bennett giggled. Gracie couldn't help but giggle, too.

. . . .

Just because Gracie and Bennett were having fun did not mean they forgot about mama bird. They knew they could help her babies by making sure they had what they needed so the daddy bird could take care of them. When we're sad, it is good to help others.

How do you think Gracie and Bennett felt as they made sure the daddy bird had food and water for the babies? Is there someone you might be able to help? What could you do?

. . . .

"Can we name the baby birds, Mama?" Gracie asked.

"Yes, as long as you understand, when the babies are strong enough, they will fly away."

Gracie and Bennett stared at their feathered friends and tried to think of the perfect names.

"I've got it," Gracie announced. "Let's name one Sky since that's the goal, to fly into the sky. And, we should name another one Zoe because I just learned in school that 'Zoe' means life, and we want them to live."

"What about the third baby bird?" Bennett asked.

"How about Hope?" Gracie asked. "Because everybody needs hope."

Bennett smiled. "I think Mama Bird would like that."

Names are important. Your name is important. Sometimes we are named after other people who were special. Other times our parents just liked our name. It doesn't matter how you got your name, just that you know it makes you special.

Look up what your name means. *What does your name say about you?*

As days turned to weeks, the baby Cardinals grew stronger.
Gracie knew it wouldn't be long before they were ready to
leave their nest forever.

"You know we are going to have to say goodbye to them soon,"
Gracie told Bennett.

"But I don't want them to go!" he cried.

"I know it's hard to say goodbye," Mama said.
"Just like it was hard when we had to say goodbye to the mother bird.
But it's almost time for them to fly."

It is hard to say "goodbye" to those we love and care about. Gracie and Bennett had done all they could to make sure the birds had food and water and now it was time for Sky, Zoe, and Hope to live the life they were born to live.

Just like the baby birds had new adventures ahead of them, (name of loved one or pet) would want you to live a happy and full life.

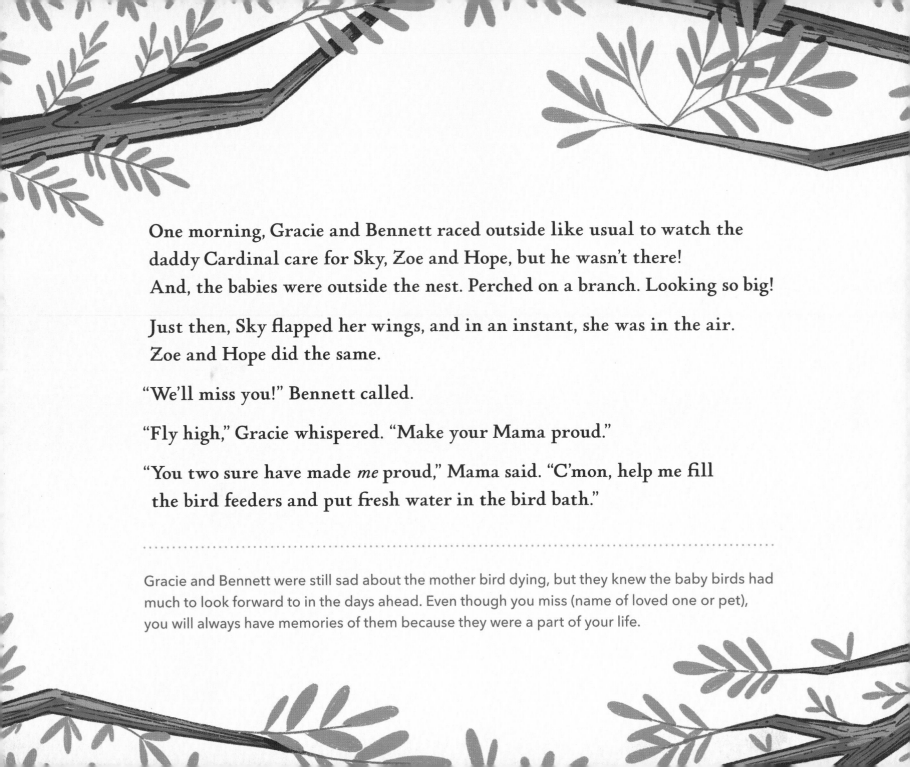

One morning, Gracie and Bennett raced outside like usual to watch the
daddy Cardinal care for Sky, Zoe and Hope, but he wasn't there!
And, the babies were outside the nest. Perched on a branch. Looking so big!

Just then, Sky flapped her wings, and in an instant, she was in the air.
Zoe and Hope did the same.

"We'll miss you!" Bennett called.

"Fly high," Gracie whispered. "Make your Mama proud."

"You two sure have made *me* proud," Mama said. "C'mon, help me fill
the bird feeders and put fresh water in the bird bath."

. . . .

Gracie and Bennett were still sad about the mother bird dying, but they knew the baby birds had
much to look forward to in the days ahead. Even though you miss (name of loved one or pet),
you will always have memories of them because they were a part of your life.

*What adventures do you think you
might like to have as you grow up?
What are your hopes
and dreams?*

That night, Gracie and Bennett crawled into their blanket tent.

"I miss Sky, Zoe, and Hope already," Bennett whispered.

"Me, too." Gracie said. "But it makes my heart smile knowing they are happy. Doing what birds do. Flying free. Flying high."

"Gracie, do you think Mama bird knows we watched over her babies, and that they're okay?" Bennett asked.

"Absolutely," Gracie answered. "Absolutely."

Caregiver's Note

It takes time to heal from the loss of a loved one or to deal with a tragedy, and it's okay to feel sad. Choosing to trust and let go of the pain allows children to remember good times and eventually understand that life goes on.

After all the *shock, denial, sadness, bargaining* and *anger,* children learn to live their lives in a *new way,* with precious memories of their loved one. They learn it is okay to be happy. They *accept* the loss, and in time, heal.

Like Sky, Zoe, and Hope flew high into the sky to their new lives, it is important to remind children that, while their loved one will be missed, they can always keep memories in their heart—and that way, they will never be far apart.

In memory of Phil Holiday, Dad to my lifelong friend Raegan Holiday Quan.
Phil lost his battle with COVID in 2021, but we are thankful he is now flying high
with his precious wife Patsy by his side once again. Loved them both.
-Michelle "Missy" Medlock Adams

Dedicated to my grandchildren Elizabeth, Matthew, Troy, and Trent.
May your hopes and dreams guide you to soar. You are in my heart always.
-With much love, Grandma Jan

Fly High

Copyright © 2022 by Michelle Medlock Adams and Janet K. Johnson
All rights reserved.

No part of this work may be reproduced or transmitted in any form or by any means, electronic or mechanical, including photocopying and recording, or by any information storage or retrieval system, except as may be expressly permitted by the 1976 Copyright Act or in writing from the publisher. Requests for permission can emailed to info@endgamepress.com.

End Game Press books may be purchased in bulk at special discounts for sales promotion, corporate gifts, ministry, fundraising, or educational purposes. Special editions can also be created to specifications. For details, contact Special Sales Dept., End Game Press, P.O. Box 206, Nesbit, MS 38651 or info@endgamepress.com.

Visit our website at www.endgamepress.com.

Library of Congress Control Number: 2022932663
ISBN: 978-1-63797-013-3
eBook ISBN: 978-1-63797-014-0

Book design by TLC Book Design, *TLCBookDesign.com*
Cover by Tamara Dever; Interior by Monica Thomas

Illustrated by Beth Snider

Printed in India
10 9 8 7 6 5 4 3 2 1

Hope

Wood-
Pecker

Dove

Blackbird

Blue
Jay

Mother